MW00749089

SKIN

That SLIMES and SCARES

Diane Swanson

CONTENTS:

GREYSTONE BOOKS

Douglas & McIntyre Publishing Group
Vancouver/Toronto/New York

No blistering and peeling for these sunbathers.
A hippo's skin makes its own sunscreen.

ALL KINDS OF SKIN

It's a good thing you were born already wrapped up in skin. That's what helps keep your insides in—and the outside out. Skin also helps protect your body from wear and tear, and heat and cold. Of all the organs you own—including your heart, lungs, and liver—your skin is definitely the biggest. On many adults, it weighs about one-twelfth as much as a whole human body.

The skin of the Australian thorny devil helps it drink. Tiny grooves collect dewdrops and channel them to the lizard's mouth.

The skin of a hippopotamus is even heavier—about one-fifth of the animal's weight. Not only does skin shield the hippo, it also guards against burning. Africa's scorching heat would dry and crack the nearly hairless skin if it didn't ooze droplets of a reddish-brown liquid. This oily liquid moistens the hippo's skin, screening it from strong sunshine. Sometimes, it also kills germs and heals wounds. The sunscreen would work on you, too—if you could convince a hippo to share!

Skin doesn't have to be thick to be tough. The rubbery skin that stretches across the arms and fingers of bats is thin, but strong. It doesn't tear easily and is very quick to mend. The skin forms wings so that a bat—which is a mammal, NOT a bird—can zoom through the night skies. On some kinds of bats, skin also joins the tail to the back legs, making flying and turning even simpler. Unlike most of the bat's body, the skin on the wings and tail flaps is bare. Hair would slow down the animal's flight.

The wrinkles in the skin of an elephant's lower legs are as unique as the grooves in your one-of-a-kind fingertips.

When the flying dragon of Asia leaps off a branch, it spreads two flaps of skin and g-l-i-d-e-s.

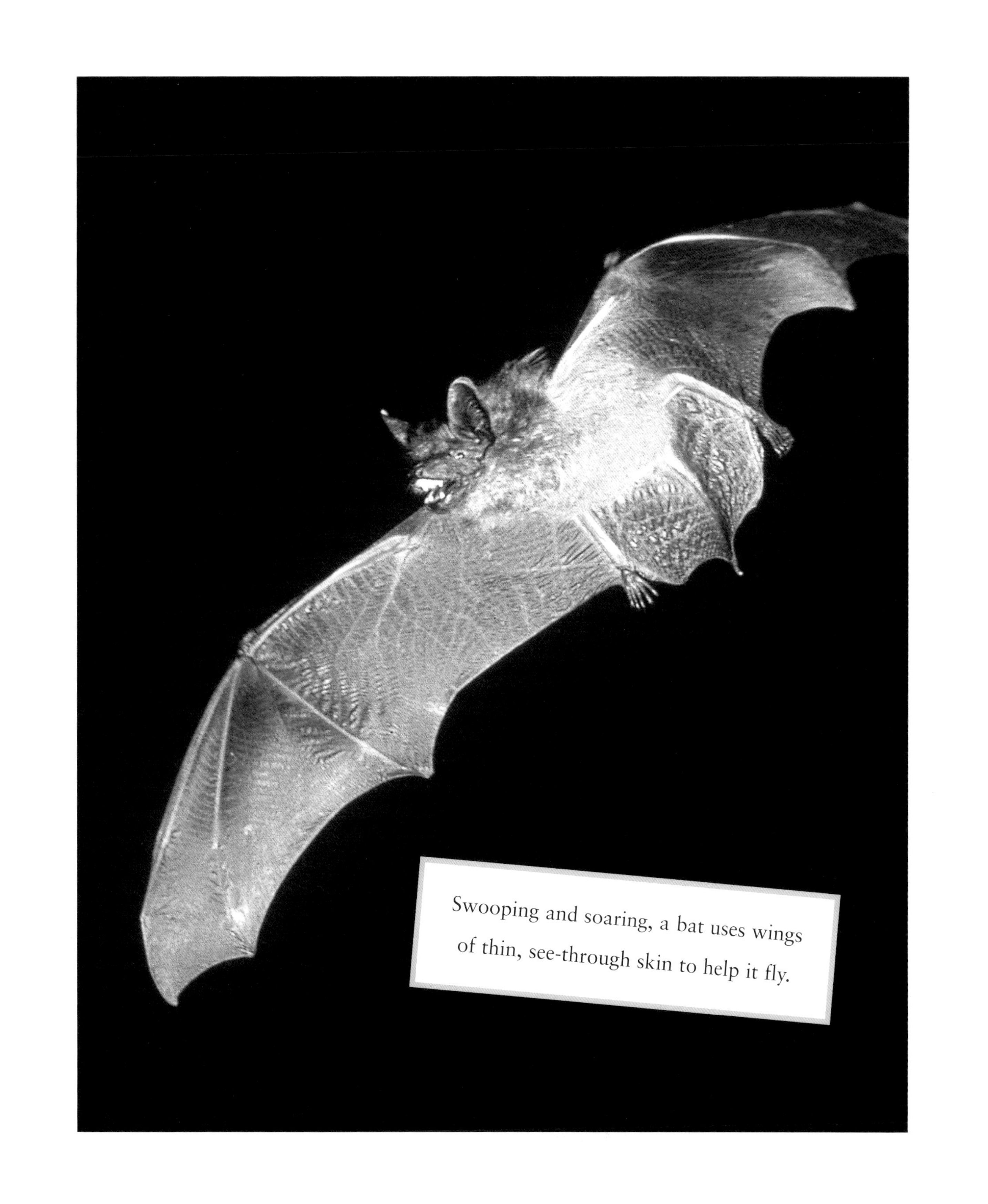

Swooping and soaring, a bat uses wings of thin, see-through skin to help it fly.

Flakes of skin from his armorlike hide mark the territory of a male white rhinoceros of Africa. Other rhinos can smell the flakes he rubs off.

Armored Skin

People may call you "thick-skinned" if your feelings aren't easily hurt. But like other human beings, you're mostly thin-skinned. Body parts that get plenty of wear—such as the bottoms of your feet—grow thicker skin, but overall, your covering is less than 6 millimeters (1/4 inch) deep.

Skin that helps protect animals from their enemies is much thicker. The hide on an elephant's back and parts of its head is four times thicker than yours. And the rhinoceros has skin that's at least as thick as an elephant's. Hundreds of years ago, people thought a rhino's hide was as strong as the metal armor worn by knights—but it's not. Spears and bullets can easily pierce a rhino.

The skin of the honey badger of Asia and Africa is so tough even porcupine quills and bee stingers can't pierce it.

Still, its skin helps protect it from the few animals, such as lions, that might attack it today.

Armadillos in North and South America are born with a soft covering of leatherlike skin. Gradually, it hardens into bony plates of armor that protect the animals' tops and sides. Each plate is linked to another by softer, more elastic skin. When threatened by their enemies—such as bobcats and coyotes—some kinds of armadillos pull their tails and legs under their armor. Then they lower it to the ground. Safe! Other kinds protect their soft parts by rolling up to form tough, hard balls. Armadillos can also take cover in a mass of prickly bushes. The thorns and sharp twigs, which don't pierce their armor, discourage their less-protected enemies from following them.

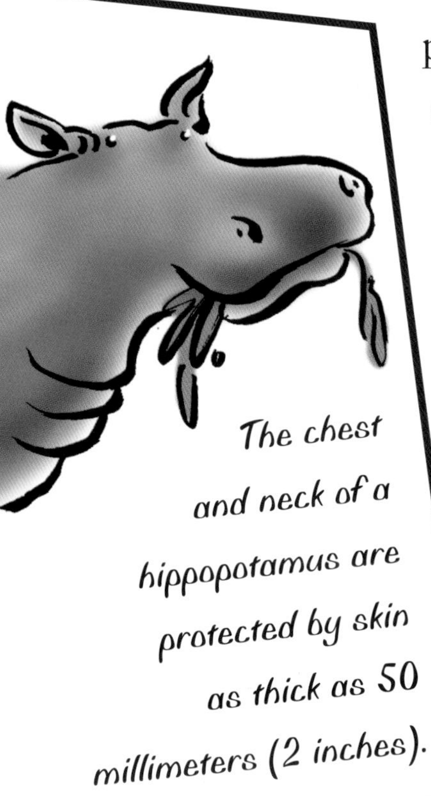

The chest and neck of a hippopotamus are protected by skin as thick as 50 millimeters (2 inches).

An African armadillo lizard has skin with prickly scales. When in danger, it forms a hoop—sticking its tail in its mouth.

Imagine swimming with all this armor!
The nine-banded armadillo avoids sinking
by swallowing enough air to fill its insides.

Pop a hagfish into an ice cream pail full of water and it quickly turns most of that water to slime.

Slimy Skin

Thanks to a layer of sticky gloop, or mucus, the skin in your nose is always slimy. That helps trap germs that might make you sick, then you can sneeze them out. If you catch a cold, this skin gets even slimier. The extra mucus helps snare more germs—and gives you a stuffy nose.

Slime makes life easier for many kinds of animals. It helps slugs and snails cruise around gardens and up fences. It helps tree frogs climb and grip slippery leaves and twigs. It also lets fish slip quickly through the water.

Slime from just one golden poison-arrow frog can coat the tips of up to 40 arrows used for hunting in South America.

No fish makes more mucus than a hagfish does. And the slime saves its life. When threatened, the hagfish oozes huge amounts of a super-thick mucus that makes its body slippery—and deadly. Any animal that nabs the hagfish could smother in the slime. Even the hagfish itself can smother if it doesn't get rid of the slime soon after its enemy has gone. But that's simple! The fish ties its boneless body in a knot near its tail, then wriggles. As the knot works its way from tail to head, it scrapes off the slime. The hagfish may have to tie another knot and repeat the trick to get rid of all the mucus.

Slimy skin helps a big octopus squeeze through a narrow crack in a rock.

Slime helps toads and frogs breathe through their skin by keeping it moist. Mixed with a poison they produce, the slime of many toads and frogs also protects them. It can sicken—or kill—most animals that swallow it. Slow-moving toads usually depend more on this slimy protection than fast-hopping frogs do.

Toad slime doesn't bother hedgehogs. They spread some of it on their spines for protection from their own enemies.

A fat toad may be an easy catch, but it's no fun to lick. Swallowing the slime on its skin can make many animals ill.

Red, pointy, and mad! This giant Pacific octopus is using its skin to say: "Swim away—now."

WARNING SKIN

Glare at yourself in a mirror. See how the skin on your forehead wrinkles and bunches up around the inside corners of your eyebrows. Your skin is pulling itself into a warning. "Bug off!" it says.

An octopus can issue warnings, too. Sometimes it draws up the skin above its eyes, forming sharp peaks. They can look a lot like pointed horns. "I'm mad," is the message. "Watch out!"

Warnings from octopuses can also be in color. Their skin contains millions of tiny, elastic cells filled with red, yellow, orange, or black chemicals. The octopus can open these cells a little or a lot, showing different amounts of the colors

When two male anoles (uh-NO-leez) meet, they puff out their throat fans of colorful skin. That's a warning to take off.

inside. And it can open them in different combinations to make patterns. A split second is all an octopus needs to change its color completely. But just what it's saying depends on the kind of octopus it is. Some kinds turn deep red to yell, "Go!" And some males tell other males to get lost by producing striped patterns.

The bright colors and beauty of many animals, including orange monarch butterflies, are warnings that they're bad to eat. Some animals are even poisonous to touch—and the fancy red lionfish is no exception. It's lovely to look at, but painful to hold. Long spines in the tall fins along its back are needle-sharp and packed with poison. So mind the skin's message: hands off!

Bands of yellow or orange on the skin of a Gila (HEE-la) monster warn other animals that it's poisonous.

Red salamanders issue a phony warning. Their skin is colored to make them look like poisonous red-spotted newts.

Beware: this beauty is a beast—a poisonous one. As it hunts among coral reefs, the red lionfish is best left alone.

Just peel and eat! When it outgrows its
skin, the anole can make a meal out of it.

TASTY SKIN

Every day you shed skin—dead cells so small you need a microscope to see them. In a single minute, you can cast off 30 000 to 40 000 of these cells. When a number of them clump together as flakes, they're called dandruff. But to house-dust mites, dandruff is dinner. These tiny eight-legged relatives of the spider gobble up a lot of dead skin. They might wait for a fungus to strike the dandruff first, to reduce the amount of fat in it.

In North and South America, little tree-living lizards called anoles eat their own skin—along with a daily diet of insects. Like other reptiles, anoles are covered in scales formed by small folds of skin. The scales on anoles are small, and

A hungry cockroach will eat just about anything—even a hunk of cast-off lizard skin.

the skin is soft. As the animals grow, they shed this outer layer of skin, but it's still loaded with protein. The anoles, like some other kinds of lizards, often eat it up.

Each year, male moose in North America sprout antlers covered with soft skin, called velvet. This skin is so rich with blood that it's warm to touch. When the antlers stop growing, the velvet dies and starts peeling off. The moose help remove it by rubbing their antlers against trees and bushes. They can often shed the velvet within 24 hours, but some strips may hang on for weeks. The skin makes nutritious meals—sometimes for the moose themselves. Small animals, such as mice and insects, also eat it. Even jays clean up strips of velvet left hanging on bushes. Yum!

Tiny insects called chewing lice nibble the scaly skin on the feet of pigeons and peacocks.

Many frogs use their mouths to yank off their old skin—full of nutrients—and eat it at the same time.

Strips of dead skin from the antlers of a moose make healthful meals.

Boo! The frilled lizard uses a wide collar of skin to make its head look bigger—and more frightening.

SCARY SKIN

Your skin isn't frightening, but you can use makeup to create an evil-looking face. Actors do it all the time. So do some witch doctors, who try to scare away whatever they believe is making their patients sick.

Some animals have skin that is naturally frightening. The South American false-eyed frog tries to spook its enemies with big phony eyes on the skin that covers its back. The frog presses its legs tightly against its body and puffs itself up, making its back look like a staring monster.

If the Australian frilled lizard can't escape trouble, it tries to scare it away. It faces its enemy, whips its tail back and forth, opens its mouth wide, and pops out a wide frill

The second pair of "eyes" on the skin of a four-eyed turtle shocks its enemies, giving the turtle time to hide.

of skin all around its head. The effect is startling! Suddenly, the lizard looks much larger—and much fiercer—than it really is.

The leathery skin on sharks is covered with thousands of sharp, toothlike scales. Now that's scary! The scales, called denticles, are built a lot like your teeth. They have ridges, grooves, and points, plus a tough outer coating. On some sharks, the toothy skin is so rough it can scrape patches of skin off any animal it contacts. Although a shark keeps growing, its denticles do not. Instead, bigger ones replace smaller denticles throughout the shark's life. Lost or broken denticles are also replaced, keeping these speedy tanks of toothy skin in tip-top shape.

In an instant, the skin of an octopus can form fake "eyes," frightening an attacker.

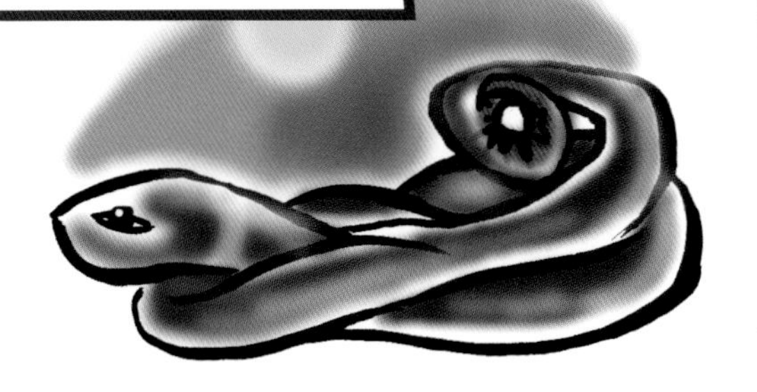

A North American ringneck snake startles an enemy by exposing bright red or orange scales beneath its tail.

You're smart to be afraid of the skin on this shark. Just brushing against its toothy scales could be a painful experience.

Hanging out in trees is a good move for the green tree python. Its leafy green skin helps it blend with the rain forest.

DISGUISING SKIN

You don't count on your skin to help you hide. But clothing—your artificial "skin"—can blend well with what's around you. Lie on the grass when you're dressed all in green and you can be very hard to spot.

Many animals depend on their skin to disguise themselves. The dirt-colored skin of huge hippos makes it easier for them to "disappear" in muddy rivers. And an alligator's skin makes the animal look like a floating log, helping it creep up on dinner.

In the tropical rain forests of New Guinea and northern Australia, a green tree python survives by having the right shade of skin. Wrapped around a tree branch, it looks like a clump of leaves.

The spanworm caterpillar is brown and bumpy. Hanging stiffly from a branch, it looks just like a twig.

Nestled in a green fern, it disappears from view. The python can rest undisturbed all day, then hunt for dinner after dark.

Day or night, it's easy to mistake a stonefish for a rock. Brown and gray skin covered with warts make this fish of the Indian and Pacific Oceans look like a bumpy stone. And thin flaps of skin on some kinds of stonefish imitate algae, which often grows on rocks. To complete its costume, the stonefish may let other animals, such as sea anemones, settle on its skin. The object isn't to hide from its enemies—it protects itself with sharp spines that inject a deadly poison. Instead, the stonefish fools animals into swimming close enough to be eaten by the "rock."

Flounders can change the color and texture of their skin to match different patches of the sea floor.

Skin that's several shades of gray helps one North American frog disappear when it flattens itself against tree bark.

Be careful not to step on this rock!
It's a poisonous stonefish in disguise.

INDEX

01 02 03 04 05 5 4 3 2 1

Greystone Books
A division of Douglas & McIntyre Ltd.
2323 Quebec Street, Suite 201
Vancouver, British Columbia, V5T 4S7

Canadian Cataloguing in Publication Data
Swanson, Diane, 1944–
Skin that slimes and scares

(Up close series)
Includes index.
ISBN 1-55054-817-4 (bound).—ISBN 1-55054-852-2 (pbk.)

1. Skin—Juvenile literature. 2. Body covering (Anatomy)—Juvenile literature. I. Title. II. Series: Swanson, Diane, 1944– Up Close
QL941.S92 2001 j573.5 C00-911211-1

Library of Congress Cataloging-in-Publication information is available.

Packaged by House of Words for Greystone Books
Editing by Elizabeth McLean
Cover photograph by Glen & Rebecca Grambo/First Light
Cover and interior design by Rose Cowles
Photo credits: p. ii Michele Burgess/First Light; p. 3 A. Maywald/First Light; p. 4 Larry J. MacDougal/First Light; p. 7 Henry Ausloos/First Light; p. 8 Phil Edgel; p. 11 Ron Watts/First Light; p. 12 Royal British Columbia Museum; p. 15 Kelvin Aitken/First Light; p. 16 Robert Lankinen/First Light; p. 19 Thomas Kitchin/First Light; p. 20 Wayne Lynch; p. 23 Kelvin Aitken/First Light; p. 24 Glen & Rebecca Grambo/First Light; p. 27 Kelvin Aitken/First Light

Printed and bound in Hong Kong.

The publisher gratefully acknowledges the support of the Canada Council for the Arts and of the British Columbia Ministry of Tourism, Small Business and Culture. The publisher also acknowledges the financial support of the Government of Canada through the Book Publishing Industry Development Program.